A DOLLHOUSE FOR CHRISTMAS

ALEESE HUGHES

ISBN: 9798499012659

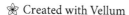 Created with Vellum

For the Hughes Family—the family that welcomed me with open arms. I love you all!

CONTENTS

The snow fell in piles rather than flurries, threatening Andi's drive home from work. She leaned forward in her seat and pressed her chin against the steering wheel as she tried to peer through the heavy snow.

Andi whispered a silent prayer under her breath, begging the Lord to offer her safe passage and a timely arrival to pick up Grace from Sarah's house. The snowstorm had lasted for a record three days in Bullman, Missouri, and she had already heard of five car accidents in just the first day on the news. And the snow was only falling harder. William had always done the dangerous driving. Andi was one to feel anxious and stressed driving in hazardous conditions.

Andi bit back the tears as she pushed on and turned right on her exit off the freeway. The hills she drove over on the way to her neighborhood made Andi even more nervous than the freeway had. She felt her car's tires slide over the large piles of snow covering the roads.

With a sigh of relief, Andi slowly pulled in at the curb just in front of Sarah's house. The car gave a worrisome shudder as the engine sputtered to a stop.

Just another thing to add to the list. How am I supposed to pay for fixes to our car? Andi thought as her lip gave a slight tremble.

Andi climbed out of the car and clenched her teeth as her sneakers sunk through the mound of snow littering Sarah's front yard. Her shoes immediately filled with the snow that would eventually melt and soak her socks. She hugged her coat tighter, trying to ignore the chill air coming through the growing hole in the back of her coat. A new coat was just one of many things she wished she could afford.

The door opened before Andi could lift a hand to knock. The simple wreath hanging above the eye hole nearly fell off its hook as the door flew open.

"Mommy!"

Andi felt warmth pierce the cold numbness the snow had given her as her daughter ran into her arms.

"Oh, Grace! I missed you! How was your day?"

Grace squeezed her face into her mother's stomach and giggled.

"It was so good! Sarah and I made cookies. She also helped me write my letter to Santa!"

"That sounds fun." Andi glanced through the narrow hallway and saw Sarah peeking her face from around the corner. "Was she good today?"

Sarah nodded and moved to join in on the group hug. "So good. Like always."

Grace wriggled out of the embrace and pushed out her lips. "You guys were squeezing me too tight!"

Sarah giggled and rubbed a hand over the little girl's blonde curls. "We just love you too much, I guess."

"Grace, go grab your coat," Andi said. Her daughter darted away.

"I'm so sorry," Andi continued in hushed tones. "My hours have increased a lot for the holiday season, but I promise I won't have to leave her with you this late every night."

"Oh, Andi." Sarah wrapped her arms around Andi once again. "Please. don't apologize. You're my best friend, and I'm happy to watch that angel of yours *any* time."

Andi had been friends with Sarah since they were freshmen in high school. Sarah was always one to help Andi and be there for her in any way she could—but it was *especially* that way after Sarah's divorce. Watching Grace and being a friend for Andi was something Sarah relied on at this point to stay sane.

"I found it, Mommy!" Grace's high-pitched voice sounded from the direction of the living room.

"All right. Let's get going, then."

"Are you sure you don't want to stay the night?" Sarah whispered, knowing that if she said it loud enough for Grace to hear, the child would demand a sleepover at all costs.

"No, Sarah, we—"

"Andi, the storm is beginning to turn into a blizzard. You know how hard it is to be driving out in this right now."

"Sarah, we only live a few streets down. We'll be okay."

"Are you sure? I know that these couple years with your husband gone have been hard. If you slide off the road or lose power, I want to make sure you two are okay."

Andi grabbed Sarah's hands and stared intently into her worried eyes. "We are going to be fine. Besides, it's not like I don't have a cell phone. I'll call you if something happens.

Come on, Grace!" Andi called before Sarah could argue any further.

"Coming!"

* * *

"HOW WAS THE RESTAURANT TODAY, MOMMY?"

Andi set the storybook down on Grace's pink quilt and smiled at her. "Oh, it was fine."

"Did your boss yell at you this time?"

Andi cocked her head to the side. "Uh, no. My boss has always been nice to me."

"I'm talking about the other one, Mommy. The one you work for during the day."

Andi resisted the urge to run a hand through her hair in worry. "I actually don't have that job anymore, sweetie. I have a new one. At Santa's Workshop downtown, remember?"

Grace shot straight up in her bed, gray eyes growing wide. "Wait, what? You work for Santa?"

"Did I not tell you? I started this week. I play an elf during the day, and I still am a waitress at the diner at night."

Grace clapped her hands together and

bounced up on down on the mattress, making the old bed springs creak.

"Mommy, this is *wonderful*! You can give Santa my letter!"

Andi winced. "Yes, right. The letter asking for that dollhouse."

Grace nodded so quickly, Andi feared she might get whiplash.

"I'll do my best, sweetie."

"Maybe *I* can talk to him and give him the letter! When is your next day off?"

Andi couldn't help but chuckle. She stroked Grace's cheek. "I'll take you to see him next Monday. How's that?"

She leaned forward to plant a giant kiss on Grace's forehead. As she did so, the tall lamp at the corner of Grace's room flickered until it went off and plunged the two of them into darkness.

"Looks like we lost power after all," Andi muttered.

"Mommy, I'm scared!"

Andi felt Grace's body leap off the mattress and onto her lap.

"Don't worry. I'm right here."

The two of them slid under the covers

13

and squeezed in close to one another. Andi wrapped her arms around her little girl and buried her nose into her soft hair.

"I love you, my bumble bee."

Grace giggled at her pet name. It was something her father had coined after seeing two-year-old Grace flitting about every flower in the backyard like a bee.

When Grace was five, William had died of cancer. And then it had just been Grace and Andi against the world. Oh, how Andi missed him. But she wasn't about to cry. At least, not until Grace fell asleep. She waited a few moments before Grace's breathing grew slow, then slowly pulled her arm out from under her and snuck off the bed.

Just as Andi began to tip-toe away, the lights flickered back on. She squinted against the sudden brightness and held her breath as she waited to see if Grace would stir. Grace's eyelids fluttered, but she remained sound asleep.

Andi breathed a sigh of relief and moved to flick the light switch but was stopped in her tracks by the sight of a small envelope with the name "Santa" penciled across the top in Grace's messy handwriting. It rested atop Grace's pink dresser that matched the bedframe and windowsill in the room—all thanks to Andi's crafty husband.

Unable to resist her curiosity, Andi made her way to the dresser and lifted the envelope in front of her eyes. Turning it around to see the back, Andi smiled when she saw the envelope hadn't been sealed yet. With a guilty look in her daughter's direction, Andi pulled the thin sheet of paper from the envelope.

With a quick scan over the letter's contents, Andi could immediately see Sarah's hand in helping Grace. The letter was typed, and the grammar was immaculate. Grace wasn't a terrible writer, but she was still only seven. Andi ran a finger over the page to smooth out the folds and began reading:

DEAR SANTA,

My name is Grace, and I am seven years old. I'm sure you already know that, but I know you get lots of letters every year and you're getting old. I'd think it might start getting harder to remember everybody.

Anyway, Mommy says that sometimes you can get really busy at the North Pole, and that there are lots of other kids out there who need presents more than I do. I understand that, so I won't be angry if you help other kids instead of me. But if you DO come, I just want one thing.

Mommy and I were walking downtown the other day, and I saw the most BEAUTIFUL wooden dollhouse in one of the store windows. It was light purple with the prettiest flowers painted all over its edges. And it was giant. It was like a castle for little dolls. Mom said it was a lot of money, and it might be hard for her to get

ME THIS YEAR, BUT I THOUGHT I'D
ASK YOU!

I'M TRYING NOT TO GET MY HOPES UP,
BUT I'VE HEARD SO MANY AMAZING
THINGS ABOUT YOU! IF YOU CAN TRAVEL
THE ENTIRE WORLD IN ONE NIGHT, MAYBE
YOU COULD GET ME THIS DOLLHOUSE.

I LOVE YOU, SANTA. AND THANK YOU
FOR THAT BARBIE DOLL LAST YEAR! ALL
SHE AND HER FRIENDS NEED IS A
HOME NOW.

LOVE,

GRACE QUINN

ANDI RUBBED a hand along her forehead.
Christmas was close, and Andi had no idea
how to give Grace the Christmas she deserved, let alone a century-old dollhouse
priced at two hundred dollars. But Grace
never asked for *anything*. That made the
letter all the more heart-breaking for Andi
to read.

The tears Andi had held back before
finally began to spill down her cheeks.

CHAPTER 2

*T*he following two mornings only brought bills, bills, and more bills. That's all Andi ever got in the mail. She tore through the envelopes and sank lower in her chair each time she saw a high balance. Taking a deep breath, she lifted the one she felt wariest about: the electric bill. She knew the cold winter days would have their toll on the final number.

With trembling fingers, she pulled the tab open and slid the paper out and in front of her eyes.

"Oh no," she said aloud, dropping the bill and putting her face into her hands. "How am I going to buy that dollhouse--let alone *anything* else?"

Christmas was only three weeks away, and she had too many debts and expenses to be able to give Grace any gifts. Andi was working two jobs, often into the late hours of the night, but neither paid her enough to handle all the expenses. They were barely scraping by. William made good money while he was alive—that is, *before* he got sick. And after many hospital bills for his treatments and check-ups, William's life insurance only helped Andi pay off the outstanding medical bills.

Andi considered moving out of the large house and downsizing but leaving the house William had built for their family seemed out of the question. But maybe she needed to start rethinking her priorities.

Andi glanced up at the digital clock on the kitchen counter. She gasped.

"It's 7:30 already?" Andi leaped from her wooden seat and hurriedly tucked the bills away into the drawer by the fridge that was already brimming with past-due amounts from the month prior.

"Grace! You're going to be late for school!"

"Mom, where's my lunch box?!"

"I put it in the fridge last night, bee. I packed it up with food already."

Grace ran down the stairs, skipping every other step and making Andi's heart nearly pound out of her chest each time.

"How many times have I told you to go down the stairs like a normal person?"

"My teacher says that we should always do everything we can to *not* be normal."

Andi sighed and gestured Grace to follow her out the front door. "I think your teacher wants you to be extraordinary. There's a difference between that and 'normal.'"

Grace skipped over the threshold and into the snow. The snowstorm had stopped a couple days ago, and the snow had started to melt, but Andi learned rather quickly that her driveway was still slick as her shoes slid as she walked.

Andi's hand slipped twice as she tried to grip the door handle of her ten-year-old minivan, now more of a dingy gray than its original white. Finally, she was able to open it and slide into her seat. Grace was a little quicker, and she jumped into the passenger seat with the reflexes of a cat.

"Uh-uh. Back."

"But Mom!"

"No. You know the family rule. Thirteen-years-old, *then* you can sit in the front."

Grace's eyes, the soft brown eyes she got from her father, grew about ten sizes, and she stuck out her lip in a pout. "But that's a whole six years away! Please, Mommy."

Andi shook her head and tried to hide the smile threatening to spread across her face.

"No."

Grace rolled her eyes and, with a groan, climbed over into the back seat, smacking her mother with her backpack along the way.

"HAVE A NICE DAY AT SCHOOL, sweetie! Just over a week before Christmas break!"

Andi waved her hand out of the car. Grace whirled around, sparkly backpack gleaming in the daylight, and flashed a smile back in her direction.

"Love you!"

Andi grinned. "Love you, too!"

And then her little girl, shorter than average for her age, quickly disappeared in the crowd of other elementary school students.

Andi sat in the parents' parking lot for a moment longer. She always felt a little empty when Grace wasn't with her—especially without her husband there.

I can't believe it's almost been two years, Andi thought. Just two days before Christmas would mark the anniversary of William's death.

Andi took a deep breath and pushed the image of her sweet husband looking so sickly and pale on that day. She switched her car into gear and made her way to work.

CHAPTER 3

"Welcome to Santa's Village! If you make your way to your right, you will find the line to sit on Santa's lap. If you have already visited with him, you'll find your pictures on the left."

Andi's cheeks hurt from smiling for so long, and the scripted words were beginning to feel like a heavy syrup in her mouth.

The parents in front of her were reeling in their rowdy children with looks of horror on their faces as their toddlers shoved handfuls of fake snow in their mouths.

"She said go right to see Santa, honey," the mother snapped at her husband.

Without even a glance in Andi's direction, she and her husband corralled the kids into the line.

Andi let out a long breath and leaned against one of the fake candy cane poles. The mall was busy, especially with Christmas just over two weeks away. People were running around in search of the perfect gifts or making their way to talk with Santa before he made his Christmas Eve trip.

She pulled at the green stockings on her leg and tried to scratch a spot that'd been itching for the last three hours. In the last two years, Andi had found herself amazed by the things she was willing to do to keep a roof over her and Grace's heads.

"Andi, I need you to take a turn next to Santa!"

Andi jumped to attention at the sound of the manager's loud voice. Linda, with a pinched expression on her narrow face, made her way to where Andi stood.

"The elf in that station must have caught something because he nearly threw up all over Santa's sleigh. I need you to take point."

Linda always talked about the duties of Santa's Village like they were just that: duties of war that had to be fulfilled, or they would have an unwanted battle of screaming children and angry parents on their hands.

"Yes, ma'am." It took every ounce of restraint Andi had not to give the short woman a mocking salute.

Andi tip-toed her way past the long line of antsy parents and excited children and stood next to the plastic sleigh that the actor playing Santa sat upon. The man fit the part perfectly. With a robust belly, red cheeks, and a sparkle in his deep blue eyes, Andi could see how children could believe he was really Santa.

"Hello, little elf!" he bellowed with a chuckle.

Andi gave a small smile. "Hello, Santa."

"Who's next?"

The jolly, old man winked at the rows of children standing before him. They all squealed with delight. A boy who couldn't have been much younger than Grace stepped forward. He wrung his hands together and shot a nervous glance back toward his mother who waved him on with a large grin on her face.

"And what's your name, young man?" Santa said as Andi helped the boy take a step into the sleigh.

He hesitated for a moment but took a seat on the large man's leg. "Charlie."

"Ah, Charlie." Santa brought a gloved finger to his nose. "I bet you've been a very good boy this year."

Charlie ran a hand through his dark hair. "I guess so."

"And what would you like for Christmas?"

Charlie's eyes darted to his mother. She gave him a quick thumbs-up, then brought her hands back around her phone to continue filming.

"I want a bike."

"Ho, ho, ho!" Santa's belly shook like the bowl of jelly it was. "Well, I'll definitely keep that in mind, Charlie."

The little boy clapped his hands together and smiled, suddenly not timid after Santa's kind words. He slid off Santa's lap and rushed over to his mom, explaining in excited bursts of energy how happy he was.

One child after another came and went, and the minutes ticked by so sluggishly that Andi thought she'd never be able to get out of the hot, green tunic of the elf costume.

"Shift coming to an end?"

Andi flashed a look back at Santa as she began to hurry away and in the direction of the locker room.

"Uh, yes. I have to get to my second job. You know, gotta pay those bills." She tried a smile, but the corners of her tired lips sagged.

Santa's bright blue eyes twinkled at Andi as another child climbed onto his lap. "Never give up hope, Andi Quinn. I think good things are coming your way."

Andi cocked an eyebrow. "Thank you, Santa. But how…" She was about to ask Santa how he knew her name, but the little girl on his knee was beginning to chat away about the pink play kitchen she wanted for Christmas.

He probably just saw my name on the work schedule, Andi thought as she scurried away, thrilled for once to get into her waitress uniform rather than the scratchy elf tights.

CHAPTER 4

*L*ittle Larry's Diner was always crowded this time of year. Of course, Andi knew that, and she expected it, but it didn't stop her from feeling overwhelmed and wishing more than anything for the night to come to an end. Every table dotting the white and black tile floors was packed full with one party after another, not leaving more than ten seconds for a busser to clear the dishes away and prepare a table for the next group. The heat of the chattering crowd and the steaming food was almost too much to bear after five hours.

Andi wiped a drip of sweat off her forehead and plastered on a tired smile as she made her way to her final table of the evening.

"And what can I get you, sir?"

The stout man raised his head and beamed up at Andi with a familiar twinkle in his brilliantly blue eyes.

Andi gasped. "It's you!"

"And it's you." The old man's smile grew even bigger underneath his white beard.

Andi planted hands on her hips. "What a coincidence, Mr. Claus!"

The mall Santa laughed, his large gut bouncing and threatening to knock over the round table. "Is it, though? Maybe it's fate!"

Andi pursed her lips. She didn't quite know what he meant by "fate," but she shook her head and continued to grin.

"Anything on the menu strike your fancy?"

He lifted the paper menu close to his eyes and squinted. "Do you have any milk and cookies?"

"Wow, you take your job seriously,"

Andi said with a laugh. "And let me guess, outside of the mall, you still like to be called Santa?"

"If you don't mind."

Andi's smile twitched precariously. *He can't be serious.*

"Now how 'bout those milk and cookies?" Santa—she felt weird even thinking about his desired name in her head—handed her the menu with a wink.

Andi took it from him, gave a slight nod, then scurried away, nearly slipping on the freshly mopped floor as she went.

"Do we have some cookies? That's all my last table wants," Andi called over the counter in the back.

The cooks of the little diner continued flipping away at hamburger patties and pancakes.

"That's *all* they want?" Harold, the oldest chef at the diner, shouted back over the popping and sizzling of the cooking food.

"Well, that and some milk," Andi replied with a shrug.

A chorus of laughter erupted from the servers and cooks in the kitchen.

"That's a festive table, isn't it?" Harold said with a chuckle.

Andi let out a laugh of her own. "You have *no* idea."

* * *

"HERE YOU GO, MR. CLAUS." Andi gave Santa a wink. "Tall glass of cold milk and a plate full of freshly baked, chocolate chip cookies."

She set down the cold glass and placed the cookies next to it. Santa rubbed his belly and licked his lips.

"Ah, my dear! This is splendid! Chocolate chip cookies are my favorite." He finished his sentence with a tap of his nose.

And up the chimney he rose. Andi couldn't stop finishing the "'Twas the Night Before Christmas" poem in her head.

"Will that be all?"

Santa inhaled two cookies at once, then brushed a few stray crumbs off his long beard. "This is perfect, Andi. Just perfect."

"Let me know if you need anything."

Andi gave the jolly man a quick wave and headed back to the kitchen. She found herself unable to stop her smile—even her cheeks were beginning to hurt. Crazy or not, that Santa Claus had a way of sharing his merriment with her, and she felt her spirits lift because of it.

* * *

"Have a good night, Andi!"

Andi whirled her head around to see Miranda, a local college student working as a waitress, waving goodbye as she headed out the door.

"You too, Miranda! Good luck on that final!"

The young woman blew out a large breath of air, causing her thick blonde bangs to rise as she did so. "Thanks. I need it. If I pass this test, nothing can stop me!"

Andi giggled as Miranda skipped through the door, whistling the tune to "Jingle Bells" as she went.

"Let's get started," Andi said to herself,

moving over to the small round table her friend Santa had sat at just half an hour earlier.

Andi often volunteered to bus tables at the end of a night shift, allowing everyone else to head home. Many of her colleagues were young and in college, and she felt it important they have as much time to study, rest, or do whatever a college student would do at the end of a day.

Ignoring the burning ache in her arms, she pulled a damp rag from her apron pocket and wiped the leftover cookie crumbs off of the wooden surface of the table. She found herself humming "Jingle Bells" as she worked, realizing Miranda had gotten the song in her head.

And then something caught her eye.

Andi hadn't noticed it before when taking the mall Santa's dishes away once he left, but how *could* she have missed it? A large, yellow envelope rested against the salt and pepper with fancy, giant letters scrawled across the top. The letters read "Andi."

She placed the rag back into her apron and slowly reached for the envelope. Once it was in her hands, she whistled at how hefty and thick it was.

What could be in here?

Andi gingerly ripped open the flap at the back of the envelope and peered inside. With a gasp, she pulled out a giant wad of cash held together with a rubber band.

"What in the world?" she breathed, thumbing through the money.

The wad consisted of *at least* two thousand dollars in one-hundred-dollar bills. It was enough to pay all of her overdue bills *and* get that beautiful dollhouse Grace wanted.

Right at the end of the stack of money, Andi found a green sticky note in the shape of a Christmas tree. The handwriting matched that of what was written on the envelope.

With tears in her eyes, Andi read the words:

A tip for those wonderful cookies, and for that beautiful smile of yours. I told you good things were coming your way.

-Santa Claus

CHAPTER 5

*D*aniel Smith despised traffic. There was nothing duller than sitting still behind a dozen cars full of people just as irritated as him. If only he hadn't needed to go to the grocery store today. Sundays were meant for staying at home. Daniel's seven-year-old Pontiac rattled dangerously as it idled. It took everything in him not to pound a fist into the horn. Even if it wouldn't make things move faster, it might have released some of his frustration.

There wasn't anywhere Daniel needed to go, so he was in no rush. He was on his way home from the grocery store, and he had no other errands to run. But Sundays were his day to lounge in front of the TV with a cold Coke and a bowl of popcorn—a day to ignore whatever happened in the world.

Daniel pounded a fist against the edge of his steering wheel, then rested an elbow against the driver's door. He stared out at the piles of snow covering the sidewalks and buildings in the heart of Bullman, Missouri. The snow was finally beginning to melt away after the three-day storm from last week. At least Daniel didn't have to worry about shoveling his driveway today.

Bullman, Missouri was a decent-sized town with a population of 20,000, two Walmarts, and more than a dozen different churches. At the thought of the different churches, Daniel caught his breath as he realized the church he used to attend regularly was right next to him.

How long had it been since he'd gone? Two years? Three? Ever since the band he and his friends had started together in high school had a falling out, Daniel hadn't had much desire to do anything else. He no longer had the heart to try going any-where besides the necessary occasions, like work and shopping. Church did not fall into that category of "necessity" for him.

Daniel's musical career had been every-thing to him, and his rock 'n' roll band "The Legends of Now" had almost had their big break when they were offered to open for the famous Sharee Thomas on tour. But small disagreements among the band members led to bigger ones, and soon, they all went their separate ways.

The tall building of the church loomed over Daniel's car as if urging him inside. Daniel still believed in God, and the occa-sional prayer was uttered out of his mouth. But after not having attended for so long, he worried what the other churchgoers would think about him.

The shrill sound of a horn honking be-hind Daniel made him jump. He hurriedly placed his foot back on the brake before he rolled into the shiny, silver SUV in front of him. He shot a look back at the truck be-hind him and yelled, "What?" though he knew perfectly well the driver couldn't hear him.

The horn blared again before Daniel realized the traffic light had turned green. He waited another second before pressing the gas pedal and looked once again at his old church. More honking ensued, then Daniel made a quick decision. He flicked his blinker on for a left turn. The top of the switch dangled precariously after he did so as the top began to fall out of the duct tape wrapped around it.

Daniel slowly pulled into an empty spot at the back of the church's parking lot, a spot with fewer people parked around him.

Maybe I can go in and out without anyone noticing, he thought as he slid out of the car and slammed the door shut. The driver's side door always had to be slammed if Daniel wanted it to *stay* shut.

Daniel glanced down at his stained jeans and wrinkled t-shirt. Not the typical outfit he used to wear when attending church. Just another reason he tacked onto his mental list to make sure he wasn't seen.

About two-thirds of the parking lot was full, so Daniel assumed the service had already started. He tip-toed around to the back, making sure to avoid any other late-comers. He stopped outside of the glass back door and took a deep breath, pushing his cheeks out as he held it. It had been a while since Daniel had seen through the glass panes and saw the large painting of Jesus hanging on the wall inside. Daniel had avoided the church at all costs after he stopped attending. His avoidance had to do with a lot of things, really. One, he was nervous about the judgment from the other churchgoers. And two, Daniel's faith in God was a bit shaky. He liked to think God existed, but his doubts tended to overpower his convictions on more days than not.

Daniel reached a hand out to push the door open but hesitated.

"What am I doing?" he muttered under his breath. Daniel scratched at his scalp, confused by his indecision.

"Oh, you're late, too?"

Daniel whirled around to the new

voice, heart jumping up to his throat. The voice belonged to a young girl who was maybe six. She could be seven—granted, a small seven-year-old. She wore a pretty pink dress that matched the flush in her cheeks. Her blonde curls bounced at the tops of her shoulders as she stepped up to Daniel. She flashed him a smile. He smiled back—he couldn't help it. The little smile with its one front tooth missing was a little too cute.

"I guess I am, huh?" he answered.

"Grace, what have I told you about running through the parking lot without me?" the newcomer stepped up to the little girl and placed a protective arm around her.

Daniel couldn't stop his jaw from dropping. The woman was gorgeous. She was the older, spitting image of the little girl, all except for the eyes. It was the first thing Daniel noticed about the woman: large, stormy blue eyes that seemed to glow against the porcelain white of her skin. Her golden hair cascaded past her shoulders and rested in a soft curl at the ends.

"Mommy, this is my new friend, uh…"

Grace looked up at Daniel, blushing. "What's your name?"

He chuckled. "Daniel. Nice to meet you."

Grace's mother offered a bright smile. "My daughter loves to meet new people. I hope you're not bothered."

Daniel shifted nervously underneath the woman's gentle gaze. Grace might enjoy meeting new people, but all of a sudden, he felt his mouth grow dry as Grace's mother continued to smile at him. He slowly took her small hand in his and shook it.

"Honestly," Daniel said, "I was hoping not to run into anyone. I haven't been to church in a while." He looked down again at his apparel. "And I don't normally dress like this."

He was shocked he said any of that aloud and bit his lip, hoping they wouldn't want to walk away right then and there.

The mother waved a hand dismissively. "Better late than never, right?"

"You can sit with us!" Grace chimed in.

Daniel felt his shoulders relax. "I'd love that.

"I'm Andrea, by the way," the woman said as she led them inside. "But you can call me Andi."

"Andi." Daniel grinned. "I like that. I'm Daniel."

And suddenly, as he followed behind the two, Daniel didn't feel quite as nervous as he did before.

CHAPTER 6

The organist's fingers danced along the keys as she began to play the opening hymn. The first measures of "Silent Night" rang in Andi's ears sweetly. It was her favorite Christmas song. Their church had been playing Christmas hymns for a couple of weeks now and would continue to do so all the way through and a few days after the holiday season ended.

About two hundred people made up the congregation that morning, and the many voices came in all at once:

"Silent night, holy night…" Andi closed her eyes and allowed the voices to fall into her ears like sweet honey. She didn't sing herself. She preferred listening and thinking about what was sung rather than distracting herself from the message by worrying about how she sounded.

Andi swayed to the rhythm and fought the tears threatening to spill from her eyes. What a wonderful night it must have been —the night Christ was born. Yes, it was a silent night, but the feeling of joy, comfort, and peace must have made people want to cry out with delight.

One particular voice stood out to Andi. She peeked an eye open to her right and watched as Daniel, the man Grace had be-friended, singing with a giant smile on his face. His voice was smooth and full— something about it had Andi mesmerized. The sound of his deep singing made the hairs on her arms rise. It was beautiful.

Andi continued to study Daniel as the verses continued. She'd never seen him be-fore, and that made sense because he said it had been a while since he'd attended church. She didn't blame him for that, though. After William died, Andi struggled with her faith in God for *months*.

Andi's eyes went up and down over Daniel. He had strong arms and shoulders, and his dark hair was neatly brushed save for the stray clump sticking out of the back of his head. It was silly, yet endearing at the same time. In fact, Daniel was quite handsome. Even the stained jeans and t-shirt looked good on him.

Andi's eyes grew wide, and she looked away, shaking her head. The last person she thought handsome had been her husband. He was gone, and Andi's heart had died along with him. It belonged to no one else.

Andi was so wrapped up in her thoughts that she didn't notice the music had stopped until the pastor rose and began speaking to the crowd.

"Brother and sisters…"

Andi jumped in her seat, shocked by the pastor's booming voice. She inched a little further away from Daniel and closer to Grace.

Pastor Johnson stood behind the massive, white podium set directly in front of the pews. The lights hanging from the ceiling reflected off the organ pipes behind the pastor and landed in his white hair, turning it yellow.

"I'd like to begin this service," Pastor Johnson continued, "by offering my deepest and sincerest prayers to those who have been affected by the winter storm that plagued us last week."

Andi bowed her head with everyone else and rested her clasped fingers against the wood of the pew in front of her. She listened to the comforting words of the pastor as he asked God for mercy and peace to those hurt and frightened, especially due to the blizzard.

A chorus of "Amens" resounded all around her, and Andi looked up to see Daniel staring at her. She felt her face grow warm.

Pastor Johnson nodded a thanks to the congregation and began to speak again: "While we are still on the topic of the devastating storm, there are many brothers and sisters of our church who have been severely affected. For instance, Brother and Sister Phillips' heater went out. Their house got so cold that their pipes burst and flooded most of their house."

Andi gasped. The Phillipses were the sweetest elderly couple she'd ever known. Mark Phillips had helped her with many house fixes in the past, and his wife had cooked for Andi for two weeks after William died.

"They, along with many others," the pastor said, "are in need of help. A basket will be passed around to collect any funds you can part from to help. These people are in great financial need."

Pastor Johnson gestured to a tiny, old lady with a brilliantly pink hat on. She rose from her seat at the front and began shuffling about with the wicker basket in her hands. She outstretched her hands to every row and person. Many dropped in cash, checks, even some spare change.

Andi swallowed. Hard. People in need. People with damaged homes, people with no money and feeling cold—people in more need than she. Andi dared a look at her sweet daughter. Grace clutched Andi's hands, squeezing so hard as if she feared

Andi would let go. Andi knew Grace was saddened by the heartbreak of others, especially after the death of her father. Her empathy surpassed that of many adults Andi knew.

"Mommy," Grace whispered, "I have a little at home. Do you think you can put five dollars in for me, and I can pay you back later?"

Andi clutched at her heart and felt warm all over. "Of course, bumble bee. That is so kind of you."

Andi reached around her back for her purse. She hurriedly pulled the zipper open as the lady with the basket began to approach. The contents of the purse included chapstick, a checkbook, various credit cards, and—

Andi took in a sharp breath. Buried in the folds of her black purse rested the wad of cash the mall Santa had given to her—though, she found herself wondering if he was just a "mall Santa." Andi had almost forgotten about the money from the kind man. She hadn't had time before the bank closed on Friday to deposit the money.

"Mommy, the basket's coming," Grace muttered through nervously clenched teeth. She poked Andi in the ribs as the lady with the pink hat approached.

Andi almost didn't hear Grace as she stared at the bills. A five-dollar bill sat by itself on the other side of the purse, and she found herself darting her eyes back and forth between the five and the wad of cash.

People in more need than me. She repeated the words in her head like a mantra.

Thumbing through the bills, Andi counted out just what she would need for her bills and pulled the remaining cash out —the two hundred dollars for the dollhouse. Hands trembling, she held the two hundred dollars and watched as two of her tears fell on the bills.

"Whoa," Grace breathed as she set eyes on the money in her mother's hand.

Andi winced. She should have been more discreet about it.

"I don't have *that* much money, Mom. How am I supposed to pay that back?"

"Oh!" Andi grabbed the five-dollar bill

from her purse and added it to the stack. "And this is your donation, Grace."

Andi ignored the gawking of Grace and Daniel as she hurriedly placed the money in the basket as it came. Shifting her eyes downward, she sank into her seat, praying no one else had noticed the pile of money she'd just given.

"Here." Daniel waved the old lady down and placed a twenty-dollar bill of his own on top of the rest of the money. Then, directed to Andi, he said, "That was very generous of you."

Andi merely nodded, avoiding his gaze. And it was that gaze—the stare of those deep green eyes throughout the rest of the service that made the minutes tick by agonizingly slow.

CHAPTER 7

*A*ndi was dreading going to the mall after picking Grace up from school the next day. The mall was the worst place to go with your child after surrendering the money intended to buy said child the one present she asked for. But Andi promised Grace that she would take her to see Santa on Andi's day off. And here they were. So, here they were.

"Mommy, you're hurting me."

"Hmm?"

"Mommy!" Grace ripped her hand away from Andi's and shook the feeling back into it. "You were squeezing it so tight."

Andi flexed her own fingers. "Sorry, bee."

"Are you okay, Mom?"

Andi nodded. "Yes, yes. Of course. Don't worry about me."

Yes, no worries should be directed toward Andi. Except for maybe the heartbreak she'd feel when Grace woke up on Christmas morning without any gifts.

The line was very short. The line to see Santa at the mall was always short on Monday nights. Most kids were headed to bed for a good night's sleep before school started in the morning. But the crowd of Christmas shoppers darting in and out of the stores in the mall was as big as ever—Christmas was just two weeks away.

"Is he the real Santa, Mommy?" Grace whispered as she gazed past the line and to the man dressed in red at its end.

Andi couldn't help but smile at the innocence of her daughter. Of course, she knew the real answer. Or did she? Her encounter with Santa at the diner had made her question her belief in the famous Claus. But maybe he was just a festive person who loved to help those in need.

She looked up at the current mall Santa

"ho-ho-ing" to the children climbing onto his lap. Was it the same one who had given her the money at the restaurant? No, this Santa's beard was obviously fake.

"Santa has lots of helpers," Andi replied. "He is so busy this time of year that he has a lot of other people go out for him, gather Christmas lists from all the kids, then report back to him."

Grace's eyes grew wide as she nodded in amazement. "So, he…" She nodded at the mall Santa with the padded suit. "He is one of Santa's helpers?"

"That's right."

Soon, Andi and Grace were at the front of the line, and Andi could hear the elf worker's lines much more clearly.

"Welcome to Santa's Village! If you make your way to your right, you will find the line to sit on Santa's lap. If you have already visited with him, you'll find your pictures on the left."

Andi didn't recognize the elf spouting the lines. She was a cute young woman with brown hair and dimples in her cheeks as she smiled. There were many elves hired to work at Santa's Workshop in the mall, so Andi was bound to run into some employees who worked different shifts than she did.

Grace was bouncing on the balls of her feet. "We're so close!"

Andi felt a pang in her chest, like someone thrust a knife into her heart and twisted it slowly.

Was it really a good idea for me to bring her here?

"Hello!" the mall Santa rose from his seat in the sleigh enthusiastically with arms outstretched and a grin beaming down at Grace. There was something familiar about his smile, but Andi couldn't put a finger on it.

"And what is your name, my dear?" Santa asked as Grace skipped past the fake snow and wriggled onto his lap.

"Grace Quinn, sir!"

He laughed. "Nice to meet you, Grace. And what is it you want for Christmas?"

And shuffled her feet about the linoleum floor of the mall. *This is it. This is where Grace's devastating Christmas begins.*

"Well, Santa…" Grace clasped her hands together and set them atop her knees, as if she was about to conduct some important business. "I *did* want this dollhouse. I wrote all about it in my letter to you, but I decided not to give that to you today."

Santa's eyebrow, painted a brilliant white to match the fake beard, rose. "Oh? And why's that?"

"I decided that my Christmas wish would best be spent by asking for you to help the people who need it more than I do." Grace nodded her head matter-of-factly.

Andi brought a hand up to her lips to stifle her gasp. *Oh, my darling Grace.*

Santa looked shocked as well, and he was silent for many seconds. "That is quite noble of you, Miss Quinn."

"Yes, bee." Andi's lip trembled as she outstretched her arms for Grace to run into. "Very noble."

CHAPTER 8

*D*aniel pulled off the itchy beard first, then the equally scratchy red suit. His shift had ended shortly after Grace and Andi had left. He couldn't decide if he felt grateful or sad that the two of them didn't recognize him—especially Andi. But, of course, Daniel hadn't expected them to. They had only met him once.

Daniel stared at his reflection in the men's locker room in the dark, back corners of the mall. He ruffled his dark hair and blew out a long breath of air. He couldn't stop thinking about Andi. She was beautiful, and Grace obviously kissed the ground she walked on. But where was

Grace's father? Daniel felt weird constantly thinking about a woman who was a mother without knowing if she was married or not.

"I see you met Andi Quinn."

Daniel froze. Had he spoken her name out loud to bring about this conversation? He whirled around to see another mall Santa coming in for his shift. The man was rotund and red with the biggest smile that curled up the startling white mustache atop his long beard. This Santa didn't have to do much work to fit the role.

"Uh, yes, I did," Daniel answered. "But how did you—"

"She works here, too. You're new, but I'm sure you'll probably get to work with her at some point."

The Santa (Daniel didn't know what else to call him) began pulling on his own red suit and black boots. But this costume seemed a much higher quality than the one Daniel had just taken off.

"Andi and Grace have gone through a lot the last few years," Santa continued. "Andi lost her husband and, of course,

Grace lost her father. And I know they're struggling with money this year."

Daniel scratched at his cheek. "Uh, you're sure about that last one? I saw Andi give a very generous donation to the church yesterday."

Santa laughed—it was jovial and sounded like what Daniel would imagine a Santa's laugh should be.

"Andi's always been a generous one. No matter the circumstance, and no matter how much she needs help herself."

Daniel raised a quizzical brow, and Santa gently pushed past him to comb over his beard in front of the mirror. Even the comb was Christmasy. A twinkling, battery-operated Christmas tree twinkled at the top of the comb.

"How do you know so much about Andi?" Daniel asked with a narrowing of his eyes.

"Ho, ho, ho! I've known her for her entire life!" Santa winked at Daniel and tapped the side of his round nose. "And I've known you for just as long, Daniel."

Daniel rubbed the back of his neck and

gave a nervous chuckle. "Well, uh, have a good shift." And with that, Daniel looped his arm through the strap of his bag resting on the floor, then scurried out of that locker room as quickly as he could.

They'll hire anyone these days.

DANIEL KNEW HE SHOULDN'T. It was creepy and just... wrong. But the numbers of the employees were there *for* this purpose. Well, kind of. He was really supposed to consult the list of elves and Santas to ask if anyone could take his shift if needed. But he wanted to find Andi's name and call her for a completely different reason.

Andi and Grace intrigued him. Not only had Andi given away possibly the only money she had to spare, but her daughter also seemed inclined to put others before herself. Generosity was a becoming quality for any person, and Daniel wanted to know more about them.

Daniel finally found the smooth, blue folder given to him days ago. It had taken him a good five minutes to find it. The words "Santa's Workshop Employee" were written neatly on the front in silver Sharpie. He sifted through the training papers until he found the employee contact list. He ran a finger down the line until he found it: Andrea Quinn.

Daniel pulled his phone from his pocket, nearly dropping it as the slick case slid along his fingers. He quickly dialed the numbers and held the phone to his ear. It was not until the phone rang a third time that his heart started pounding.

What am I doing? This is crazy! Daniel brought his phone down and was about to press the "end" button, but then he heard a soft "Hello?"

Daniel's mouth went dry. He smacked his lips together, trying to bring moisture back to his mouth before he dared speaking.

"Uh, hi. Is this Andi Quinn?"

There was a pause. A long pause. Daniel rubbed a hand along his face.

Stupid. I'm so stupid.

"This is she."

Her voice was sweet. He could almost picture her entrancing eyes narrowing as she awaited the revelation of her caller's identity.

Daniel chuckled. "Yes, uh, this is Daniel Smith. We met at church yesterday."

Another pause. Daniel half-expected to hear the clicking sound of Andi hanging up.

"How did you get my number?" She didn't sound angry—just apprehensive.

"Oh, this is funny." Daniel forced out another chuckle as he ran a hand through his hair. "I actually just started working as a Santa at the same mall you work at. I was the Santa you and Grace saw tonight."

The usual pause in between words became a laugh on her end.

"Small world!"

Daniel laughed along with her. "Yeah. Small world. So..." Daniel mindlessly tapped his fingers on his marble kitchen counter. "This is not any of my business, but I couldn't help but notice the donation you made yesterday."

Daniel could hear Andi sigh.

"I'm so sorry," he said quickly. "I shouldn't have called you at all. Forget I said anything."

"No, no. Don't hang up," she interjected. "I—it's okay. That was kind of a spur-of-the-moment decision. I actually…" She laughed again. "I don't know why I'm telling you this, but we don't really have a lot of money. I got a *huge* tip the other day. I used most of it to pay for my bills, and the rest was going to go to…" She trailed off.

Daniel remembered the dollhouse Grace mentioned at the mall, and the look of tears threatening to spill from Andi's beautiful eyes.

"Let me guess. A dollhouse for Grace?"

Daniel heard a soft whimper at the other end of the line.

"Yes. This *gorgeous* one on display at the antique store downtown."

Daniel opened his mouth to respond, but she continued:

"I don't know how I'm supposed to explain to her that Santa can't bring her gifts this year," Andi said. "Oh, I wish William was still here."

Daniel brought the phone away from his mouth as he groaned. He'd almost forgotten she was a widow. That mall Santa had mentioned something about it, and Daniel felt stupid for calling someone who had lost her husband.

"I'm sorry." She chuckled. "I'm rambling. William was my late husband."

Daniel heard a faint sniffle.

He pounded his forehead again and again. *Stupid, stupid, stupid.*

"I'm so sorry for your loss," he said.

"Oh, thank you. But please, don't worry about us. It was nice of you to call." Andi was speaking faster, as if she were about to hang up.

Come on, Daniel, he scolded himself. *Think of something else to say!*

"Well, I've got to go. I'll talk to you again sometime?" Andi said.

"Uh, yeah. Sure." He was about to ask her to dinner or something, but the sound of her line ending as she hung up interrupted him.

Daniel set his phone on the counter and stared at it for a good few minutes. It was idiotic of him to think he could succeed in wooing a woman after his last serious relationship ended three years ago—right before he left for tour. At the time, Daniel felt it unnecessary to have a girl waiting at home for him. They weren't married, and he didn't want to have someone pulling him away from his dreams.

I was an idiot.

Daniel was much too out of practice when it came to women—*especially* if he were to ask out a grieving widow. When had her husband died, even? Was it recent?

Daniel groaned, planted his elbows on the counter, and threw his face into his hands. There had to be *some* way he could get Andi's attention.

CHAPTER 9

*A*ndi saw him at church that next Sunday, and the next. Daniel had started taking the time to put on a button-down shirt and tie. He looked even more handsome than when she first met him. Which Andi did not like—she couldn't accept her growing attraction for Daniel. And it made it more awkward for her when Grace invited him to sit with them again.

"You look lovely today," Daniel whispered close to Andi's ear as he sat down next to her. She felt a shiver go down her spine.

"You do, too," Daniel directed to Grace

with a wink. Grace giggled and turned a bright pink.

The opening hymn started, and this time Andi sang as loudly as she could, even though she didn't enjoy singing, just to drown out the sound of Daniel's gorgeous voice.

"Brothers and sisters, the best day of the year is quickly approaching," the pastor said over his pulpit once everyone tucked their hymn books away.

"He has a stain on his robe."

Andi gave Daniel a sideways glance. "What?"

"Pastor Johnson. Look at his robe," Daniel whispered, pointing toward the pulpit.

Andi squinted her eyes as she tried to see the supposed stain, but she quickly realized she didn't need to strain to see.

"Oh, no!" Andi breathed, bringing her hand to stifle a giggle. "Was he eating a jelly donut this morning? Oh, poor pastor!"

Daniel threw his head back and laughed, forgetting to be quiet, but Andi couldn't help but snicker along with him.

"Hush!" a young mother hissed from the pew behind them. "Even my toddlers are better behaved than you two."

Andi and Daniel shared a look, both of their lips twitching as they tried not to continue laughing.

"What's so funny, Mom?" Grace said in her normal, loud voice, much to the chagrin of many. Grace tugged at Andi's sleeve to get her attention.

Andi shook her head. "Shh! Nothing. Let's just listen to the sermon."

But Andi couldn't focus on the words spoken that Sunday. All she could think about was Daniel sitting next to her and chuckling along with him through the rest of the service.

ANDI WOKE up the next morning thinking about Daniel Smith. He had called her just to chat a few more times this last week, and she was starting to feel comfortable with him. It had been a long time since a guy had called her to talk about anything other than work. She remembered Daniel's first phone call. Once the conversation had ended, she hurriedly hung up the phone, feeling frightened by the implication of the phone call, but for a short second, she also felt flattered. Even her stomach did little flips. But the feeling of excitement scared her even more than the phone call.

She looked over to her nightstand and stared at the small frame holding a picture of her sweet William—it was taken just before he'd been diagnosed with cancer. His smile was large, which made his brown eyes squint into thin lines and accentuated the wrinkles at the edges of his face. He was so happy then. And so handsome.

It had taken Andi a long time not to burst into tears every morning when she felt an empty space on their queen-sized bed after his death. And Andi knew it would take even longer, if ever, for her to feel ready to date again. But her recent interactions with Daniel threatened to make her feel differently. And Andi didn't like that.

Andi threw off her soft, warm quilt and

forced herself to roll out of bed. It had been a late night for her as she worried about a multitude of things, and now Daniel Smith was on that list of things to worry about.

"I'm ready to go, Mom."

Andi ran a hand through her ratted hair and gave a weak smile to Grace. "Great. The sooner we leave, the sooner I can get back to bed. My shift doesn't start until this afternoon."

THE DRIVE to school was much more arduous than usual. Grace knew something was bothering her mother. Andi could tell. If Grace knew her mother was worried or upset, she didn't know what to do except remain quiet. Andi was never good about talking through her feelings, and Grace hated seeing her mother upset.

The boring, conversation-less drive was not helped by Andi's exhaustion. She kept glancing at Grace's reflection in the rearview mirror. Grace continued to tap an anxious foot against the floor mats and stared at the window unblinkingly.

"You know, Grace, that was such a wonderful thing you said to Santa Claus the other night."

Grace perked up. "I thought you said he wasn't the real Santa. That he was one of his helpers."

Andi smiled. "Yes, yes. That's true. But still, that was such a generous, selfless thing you did."

Andi caught a glimpse of Grace shrugging in the mirror. "I meant it, Mommy. I'm happy even without Christmas gifts."

A trickle of warmth spread along Andi's body from her head to her toes. She must be doing something right for her child to act in such a way. Maybe she didn't have to worry too much about Santa not bringing Grace presents this year—it was almost like Grace would accept it.

Andi pulled in front of the school and craned her neck around the driver's seat to give her daughter a big smile.

"I love you so much, bumble bee. No matter what, we'll have a good Christmas.

All we need is each other. And today's your last day of school before your Christmas break!"

Grace smiled back, but her eyes shifted to the hands fumbling with the strap of her sparkly backpack.

"You're right, Mommy. I love you."

And with that, little Grace stumbled out of the car and made her way up to the school's entrance.

CHAPTER 10

*H*is audiences were generous today. Daniel was pleased to realize that as one person after another threw in bills of all denominations into his guitar case. Singing and playing Christmas carols on the street during the holiday season definitely brought in more cash than working as a mall Santa.

The streets of downtown Bullman were bustling in a way they never did any other time of the year. Every shop was packed with eager shoppers, especially grandmas "ooh-ing" and "aah-ing" at the glass dolls and other collectors' items they could get their hands on.

"This will be *perfect* for my granddaughter!" one lady with short, red hair exclaimed as she stepped out of a corner shop called "Perfection Boutique." Like most others surrounding it, the shop was covered in lights and garlands to not only fit in with the season but also to appeal to the many shoppers.

Daniel stood in the middle of it all, directly across from "Antiques for All." It was a little store with white-painted brick and a display window about as big as the shop itself. And right behind the single-paned glass stood a tall and elegant purple dollhouse. He still didn't know how he was going to lug that thing home in his tiny car, but he'd figure that out when the time came.

Daniel decided to stand in sight of the dollhouse while he performed—he knew he worked harder and better when his goal was in sight. It had been a long time since Daniel picked up his guitar and sang for a crowd. Going on a year-long tour with his band, just to have the group split up and surrender any sort of success, had been enough for Daniel to push music away for a while. But having a goal motivated Daniel to get over himself.

"Five hundred dollars for that house," he muttered again under his breath. He glanced down at the bills and few coins scattered inside his black case. He would have to count it carefully, but Daniel thought he could see at least fifty dollars inside. He would get there. He knew it.

"Silent, holy night…"

Daniel strummed the strings of his guitar with his lucky pick and sang the famous words everybody knew by heart. It was a popular one when it came to bringing in a crowd. But Daniel suddenly found himself thinking of when he sang "Silent Night" at church the first day he met Andi. When Andi stood beside him and watched as he sang. But when he looked back, she would pointedly look away and focus on something else. They'd become friendlier in the past two weeks, but he still felt guilty thinking about how she must feel about drawing close to a man again after losing her husband.

"Sleep in heavenly peace…"

Daniel shook his head and tried to pay attention to his singing. He had no right to feel offended by Andi's actions. They'd barely met, and her husband was gone. He just needed to get the dollhouse for Grace and give them both some space. Their little family deserved a good Christmas, and it was something he could give them.

"Thank you!" he exclaimed as his song finished and the crowd of shoppers clapped, and even a few wiped tears from their eyes. It was nice to sing for a crowd again. He forgot about the rush he felt when bringing people joy and making them experience raw emotion just by the sound of a well-played chord.

Daniel smiled at each person as they passed and threw some money into his case. *Just a few more days of this, and I can buy that dollhouse for sure.*

But just as he thought that, he nearly dropped his guitar on the hard pavement as he saw the antique store's window was empty.

"Excuse me," he breathed to the crowd,

shoving his guitar in the case along with all the money and roughly snapping it shut.

Case in hand, Daniel bolted to the antique store and dashed through the door, nearly bowling over an elderly couple lugging five bags each.

"Hello?" he called. Daniel didn't see any workers at the small checkout corner or around any corners by the big pieces of furniture and dusty tea sets for sale.

The sound of a curtain drawing brought Daniel a touch of hope. He rushed toward the back of the store.

"May I help you?" The voice belonged to a tall man in possibly his late fifties.

"Yes. Uh, what happened to that doll-house you had on display?"

"Oh." The storekeeper grinned. "That was a very popular item. I sold it just about five minutes ago, I think."

Daniel scratched his head. *How did I not see someone walking out with it?* Daniel knew his thoughts had been somewhere else, and he often closed his eyes as he sang. But still, five minutes was exceptionally fast for someone to leave with a cumbersome doll-house without Daniel noticing.

"Is there something else I can help you with? I have other dollhouses for sale."

Daniel anxiously tapped his fingers against his thigh. *What am I going to do now?*

"I also have a large selection of glass dolls. I don't know what the girl you're shopping for wants, but you're welcome to look."

Daniel was too stunned to reply.

"Sir?" The shopkeeper approached Daniel and outstretched an arm to tap him on the shoulder. "Are you all right?"

"Uh..." Daniel clutched the handle of his guitar case so tightly, his knuckles were turning white. "Uh, no. Thank you. I—I gotta go."

Daniel stumbled out of the shop. *There goes* that *idea.*

CHAPTER 11

There was just one week until Christmas, and Andi was beginning to panic. No matter how much Grace claimed she didn't need gifts, Andi still wanted to figure out *some* way to give Grace the best Christmas she could give her.

"Why so glum, Andi?" Sarah poked at Andi's shoulder until she shrugged it away.

"Oh…" Andi pursed her lips. "This time of year used to be my favorite."

"*Used* to?" Sarah leaned her elbows over her long dining table. "I know it's hard without William, but—"

"Yes, it is hard without him, but there's something else."

Just as Andi was about to explain, the buzzing of her phone vibrating in her pocket made her jump in her seat.

"Whoa, there." Sarah threw her head back and laughed. "It's just your phone."

Andi gave a soft chuckle. "Yeah, I know. I just don't normally have it on vibrate. I did that for work yesterday."

Andi pulled her slender phone with the bright pink case Grace had bought from the dollar store for her birthday. She stared at the screen and winced.

"What? Who is it?" Sarah threw herself across the table to try and get a look. Her eyes widened. "Who's *Daniel?*"

Andi brought her fingers to her suddenly warm cheeks. "Oh, no one. No one at all."

Sarah retreated back to her seat, but she was far from defeated. Her sly smile only grew. "Why don't you put it on speaker if it's no one?"

Andi gulped. "Uh, I think I should be picking Grace up from her friend's house. Thanks for the coffee!"

Sarah waved a finger in the air. "Not so

fast. You dropped her off for a *sleepover*. Now, you'd better hurry and answer that. It's rung five times already."

Andi brought a trembling hand to her phone's screen, clicked the green answer button, then reluctantly clicked the speaker button directly after.

"Hi, Daniel," Andi choked out. Sarah clapped her hands in excitement.

"A man!" Sarah whisper-shouted.

"How are you?" he asked.

Sarah giggled.

"I'm doing fine. A little stressed now that Christmas is so close."

"Yeah." There was a pause, and Andi could hear him nervously clicking his tongue on the other end of the line. "I was hoping that maybe I could relieve some of that stress for you."

Sarah raised an eyebrow. "Sounds romantic," she mouthed.

Andi shot her friend a look. "Oh? What did you have in mind?"

"Well, perhaps we could discuss that at dinner. Are you free tonight?"

Sarah pumped her fists in the air. "Say yes! Say yes!" she nearly shouted.

Andi placed her hand over the speaker. "Go away, Sarah."

Sarah shrugged and skipped out of the room.

"Is someone there with you?" Daniel said.

Andi rubbed at her forehead. "Uh, no. It's just me."

"So..." Daniel cleared his throat. "Dinner?"

Andi flexed her fingers. How could she say no? Daniel was so nice. Well, it was just dinner. One outing with him wouldn't hurt. Besides, he hadn't exactly said it was a date.

"Sure," she finally replied.

"Great!" Daniel's voice went up almost an octave. "Should I pick you up around six? Can you text me your address?"

"Yes and yes," Andi said.

"Then, it's a date."

Oh, no. He said it. He said "date."

"I'll see you at six!" he exclaimed just before hanging up.

Andi carelessly dropped her phone on Sarah's dining table.

What did I just do?

* * *

ANDI LOOKED like an angel sitting across from Daniel. Her yellow dress made her fair skin and golden hair glow as the yellow light of the restaurant bounced off the fabric.

"What are you getting?" Andi raised her laminated menu, which covered her soft pink lips from Daniel's view. Her hands shook slightly, but Daniel didn't judge her. He was nervous, too.

"Well, I haven't been here in years, but I really like the alfredo. If they still have it."

Andi raised an eyebrow and stifled a giggle. "This is an Olive Garden. I'm sure they still have the alfredo."

Daniel laughed and nervously ran a sweaty hand along the napkin on his lap. "Yes, of course."

Andi set her menu down again. "I'll get whatever you're having."

Daniel pulled at the stiff collar around his neck. "Sounds good."

The waiter standing at the side of their table cleared his throat.

Daniel nearly jumped out of his seat. "Oh, you're already here."

"Yes, sir. I asked you what you'd like to drink, then you got…" The waiter looked over to Andi. "Distracted."

Andi brought a hand to her mouth to hide her snicker.

Daniel mentally urged the flush in his cheeks to go away. "We'll both have some water and the chicken alfredo."

"Soup or salad?" The waiter tapped his pen on his pad in hurried movements, obviously impatient.

"What? Does that cost extra?"

Andi couldn't hold in her laugh any longer.

"No, sir. It comes with the meal."

"We'll take the salad," Andi interjected, handing her menu to the waiter.

Daniel followed suit and palmed his forehead as the waiter walked away and out of sight. "That could have gone better," he breathed.

"Oh," Andi said, waving a hand dismissively, "it was fine. Besides, he was rude."

"Yeah." Daniel clasped his hands under the table and twiddled his thumbs.

"You really haven't been to an Olive Garden in years?" Andi queried with a disbelieving raise of her slender brow. "It's one of my favorites."

Daniel looked around at the green and brown aesthetic and the fake vines wrapping around the banisters and walls.

"Yeah, it's been a long time. I don't get out much. At least, when I'm not working, anyway," he replied.

"So…" Andi set her elbows on the table, then her chin in her hands. "How can you relieve my holiday stress, Daniel?"

"Hmm? Oh, that!" Daniel shoved his hand in his suit pocket, the one holding the envelope full of the cash, but he didn't pull it out yet. "I'll explain. You—you're story really inspired me."

"What story?"

"Well… All of it, really. How hard

you work to keep Grace happy, the money you gave to the church, and the fact that you want to buy Grace that dollhouse."

Andi frowned, retracted her arms from the table and placed them in her lap, but Daniel was undeterred.

"Anyway," he continued, "I really wanted to show you how admirable you are by—well, I *tried* to buy that dollhouse for you, but…"

Daniel pulled out the envelope. Scrawled messily across the top were the words: "For Grace's Dollhouse."

"The dollhouse was gone before I had enough to buy it, but I wanted to give you what I earned. I saved up all I could spare, and I got pretty close. I *really* wish I could have bought the dollhouse, but I thought maybe the money would still be of help to you."

Daniel slid the envelope across the table, then raised his head to look into Andi's eyes. But her eyes were closed.

"Andi, are you all right?"

Andi bit her lip. She then raised her

gaze to meet his. "Who do you think you are?"

Daniel drew in a sharp breath. "What? I—"

She was standing now. "We don't need your charity. I hardly even *know* you!" Tears were spilling down Andi's face now, making her mascara smear underneath her large, beautiful eyes.

Daniel raised his hands. "I'm sorry. I didn't think—"

"You *didn't* think!" Andi cried. She pulled the purse from her cushioned seat and wrapped the brown strap across her bare shoulders. The entire restaurant's attention went Andi's and Daniel's way as she began to storm off.

Andi paused halfway past the tables, then slowly turned around. "I'm sorry, just... Please don't talk to me again." She wiped a hand across her wet nose and ran out of the front doors and into the night.

Daniel threw his head back against the booth and rubbed at his eyes. Did that really just happen?

"I'm such an idiot," he hissed underneath his breath.

"She'll come around."

Daniel blinked twice, then looked behind him and toward the new voice. "Hey! It's you!"

"Ho, ho, ho! Yes, it's me. I'm a sucker for the breadsticks here." The mall Santa that Daniel had met a couple weeks ago waved a piece of steaming bread above the wall separating their booths.

"Wow, that beard of yours really is something, huh? Does it ever..." Daniel gestured at the crumbs of the breadstick falling into Santa's white beard. "Does it ever get annoying?"

"Well, I've had *lifetimes* to get used to it." The mall Santa licked his fingers.

Lifetimes? Daniel frowned. *Maybe it's just a figure of speech.*

"I especially love it when I get pieces of cookies stuck in my beard. Ho, ho! It's always a delicious surprise later!"

Daniel couldn't help but laugh.

"But, like I was saying, I know Andi will

speak to you again. You just need the right leverage."

"And what leverage, dare I ask, do I need?"

Santa's blue eyes lit up with a mischievous glow. "I heard you saying something about a dollhouse. I have something that might interest you."

Daniel raised an eyebrow. "Oh?"

"Yes. Why don't you pack up the chicken alfredos you just ordered," Santa nodded in the direction the rude waiter had gone to input Daniel's order, "pay for them, then meet me out back."

Daniel chewed on his tongue in thought. Was it really a good idea to follow a strange, old man who insisted on being as much like Santa as possible to the back of a restaurant in the dark of night? But then he thought of Andi and how hurt she looked at Daniel's offer to give her money. If there was something he could do to mend the fences, he would do it.

In spite of himself, Daniel replied, "Okay."

CHAPTER 12

"*Y*ou bought it?!" Daniel's mouth was agape as the mall Santa lifted the trunk to his silver minivan with Christmas stickers covering almost the entirety of the car's body. Inside the trunk rested the beautiful, purple dollhouse that Grace wanted so much.

"Why?" Daniel cried. "Do you have a granddaughter or someone else to give it to? Or are you stalking me?"

Santa snorted. "I'm not stalking you. Well, not in the *usual* sense of the word. And I have lots of children to give things to if that answers your question. But this..." He gestured toward the dollhouse with its gorgeously painted windows and flowers decorating the walls. "I thought this might be a present better coming from you."

Daniel's hands dropped to his sides and tried to ignore how creepy all of that sounded. Unless he really was Santa Claus... "Are you serious?"

Santa nodded with a smile.

Daniel set the paper bag holding the al-fredos on the ground and scrambled for the envelope he'd replaced in his pocket after Andi left. "How much did you get it for? Two hundred? I can give you three." Daniel thrust the envelope out to the old man.

Santa laughed. "Fifty is fine."

Daniel's arm fell for a second. "What? But—"

"Fifty dollars. Not a penny more. Should I make it ten?"

Daniel shook his head. "No, no! I want to give you whatever I can!" He sifted through the bills in the envelope and pulled out a fifty-dollar bill.

Santa took the money and tucked it away in a back pocket. "Thank you, Daniel.

And please, we must figure out how to get this to little Grace. Allow me to help."

CHRISTMAS MORNING, six a.m. Andi sat on her ragged couch that had seen better days and continued to stare at their meager tree. A few red ornaments Andi had picked up from the dollar store hid the various bare spaces in the dwindling branches, and at least it wasn't *completely* empty underneath. Andi was able to buy a few treats and two Barbie dolls. And there was a gift from both Andi's and William's parents tucked under the branches for Grace. That would make her happy.

Andi sighed and sank further into the scratchy couch cushions, sipping her hot cocoa. She was determined not to be depressed on Christmas of all days. If anything, Grace deserved that from her mother. But just as she decided to adopt a positive attitude, Daniel popped into her mind.

She had been much too harsh on

Daniel—she knew that. He was being kind and generous, and she just threw it back in his face. Granted, the gesture had felt almost romantic, and that triggered emotions she didn't feel ready to handle. But Andi also knew her pride had gotten in the way. It had irked her to see someone else provide for her daughter better than she could.

Maybe I should call him and apologize, Andi thought.

The sound of footsteps tumbling down the stairs made Andi's heart sink. *Here she comes.*

"Mommy!" Grace said, leaping over the top of the couch and landing in Andi's arms. "Merry Christmas!"

Andi's lip trembled as she squeezed her little girl tight to her chest. Grace hadn't even tried to look under the tree.

"Merry Christmas, my sweet bee."

Grace pulled away and danced around the living room in her red and green slippers—something Sarah had bought for Grace just a few days prior. "I have something for you, Mommy!"

Andi wiped a stray tear away and smiled. "You do?"

"Yes!" Grace ran over to the kitchen, slippers sliding on the tile floor. She grabbed the stepping stool tucked away under the sink, placed it underneath a high cupboard and pulled the cupboard open. She reached an arm behind the many cans Andi hardly ever touched and pulled out a small, round package tied up in silver ribbon.

Andi brought her hands to her heart. "You didn't have to get me anything, darling."

Grace shook her head. "I *wanted* to get you something, Mommy."

Grace gingerly set the package on her mother's lap and sat, legs crossed on the floor in front of her. "Open it," she whispered, bouncing up and down. She still hadn't looked under the tree.

Andi pulled the ribbons off and slid a finger underneath the top flaps. She gasped as she caught sight of what was inside. Andi grasped the chain in between two fingers and pulled out the necklace.

"Did you make this?" The silver chain had round, purple glass beads in between every other link.

Grace shrugged. "Sarah helped me. She and I picked out the materials at the craft store, and I made the necklace. Purple is your favorite color, right, Mommy? Like me."

A lump grew in Andi's throat as she fought back tears. "You're right. Oh, bumble bee, I love it!" Andi outstretched her arms and gestured for Grace to join her in a hug.

They embraced for a minute before Andi pushed her away and pointed at the tree. "Now, go open your gifts!"

* * *

GRACE WAS JUST as grateful for her few gifts as a child who received one hundred would be. It was truly a joy for Andi to watch. What had she done to deserve such a wonderful child?

A few hours passed. They played some games, watched a Christmas movie, and then Sarah invited the two of them over for Christmas dinner.

Just as Andi was about to head upstairs to put on something cleaner and nicer, her front door burst open, and Sarah ran through it. Her nose was red from the cold outside, and her brown hair stuck up in places.

"I am here to pick you both up!" Sarah exclaimed, pushing her way past the hallway and to the living room. "Are you ready?"

Andi chuckled. "Not quite. Just give us ten minutes."

Just then, the doorbell rang.

"Whoa," Sarah breathed, staring at the door she had just slammed shut, "I didn't see anyone coming up."

Andi scratched at her head and slowly approached the door. She turned the brass knob, then gasped at the sight. A dollhouse —no, *the* dollhouse stood tall and proud on their doormat.

"Is that…" Sarah's eyes widened as she moved to stand next to Andi.

"It is…" Andi whispered.

Sarah shook Andi's arm. "Look! There's a note!"

Andi reached a shaking arm to the small, yellow sheet of paper taped to the roof of the dollhouse. Sarah shoved her chin on Andi's shoulder to read along with her. The note read:

ANDI,

I WANT TO APOLOGIZE FOR THE OTHER NIGHT. IT WAS WRONG OF ME TO THINK I COULD INJECT IN PLACES I DIDN'T BELONG. AND I HOPE THAT BY GIVING GRACE THIS DOLLHOUSE, I'M NOT OVERSTEPPING. I PROMISE I WILL GIVE YOU SPACE AND NEVER TALK TO YOU AGAIN, IF THAT IS WHAT YOU WANT. PLEASE JUST ACCEPT THIS GIFT AS MY SINCEREST APOLOGY.

I HOPE YOU HAVE A MERRY CHRISTMAS.

SINCERELY,

Daniel Smith

P.S. I can't take all the credit. I had a little help with a jolly man in a red suit. I'm sure that will make Grace excited.

Andi was speechless. She dropped the letter into the snow at her feet and brought a hand to her mouth.

Sarah jumped up and down. "I *told* you he was a good guy!"

Andi couldn't even nod. She was so shocked.

"Well, are you going to call him *now?*" Sarah pressed with hands on her hips.

Andi turned quickly on her heel and sped away to the kitchen. She fumbled through the clutter on the counters until she found her cell phone.

Her trembling thumbs found his name in her contacts, and she hurriedly pressed the phone against her ear. There were three rings before he picked up.

"Andi?" he said.

"Daniel!" Andi froze, realizing she had shouted his name then, quieter, she added, "Would you like to have Christmas dinner with us?

NOTE FROM THE AUTHOR

Thank you for taking the time to read this holiday novella! If you enjoyed it, I would greatly appreciate a review on Amazon and Goodreads.

Without readers like you, authors like me would be nowhere! So, from the bottom of my heart, thanks for reading.

Aleese Hughes is many things: a mother and wife, an avid reader, a performer, and an author. Aleese enjoys her time at home with her children and relishes the opportunities to pick up a good book or write one herself.

Having grown up around theater her entire life, Aleese has a natural ability when it comes to charming audiences while on stage. And the same goes for her knack to put words to paper and create stories that people of all ages can read and enjoy.

The fantasy genre is not only her favorite to read, but it is also what she writes. As an up-and-coming Young Adult Fantasy author, she's excited to share her stories with the world.

Learn more about Aleese Hughes and her books at aleesehughes.com or inspectormage.com.

 facebook.com/aleesehugh
twitter.com/AleeseHughes

ALSO BY ALEESE HUGHES

The Tales and Princesses Series

BOOK ONE: PEAS AND PRINCESSES

BOOK TWO: APPLES AND PRINCESSES

BOOK THREE: PUMPKINS AND PRINCESSES

BOOK FOUR: BEASTS AND PRINCESSES

After the Tales and Princesses—A Set of Novellas

NOVELLA ONE: JANICE WALLANDER: A NOVELLA
RETELLING THE TALE OF RUMPELSTILTSKIN

NOVELLA TWO: QUEEN DALIA CHAR: A
NOVELLA RETELLING THE TALE OF ROSE RED

The Inspector Mage Trilogy

BOOK ONE: INSPECTOR MAGE: BLOOD ON THE
FLOOR

BOOK TWO: INSPECTOR MAGE: THE HANGING
PRIEST (AVAILABLE IN 2022)

BOOK THREE: TBA

Printed in Great Britain
by Amazon